When the Moon Is High

By
Alice Schertle

Illustrated by
Julia Noonan

HarperCollins*Publishers*

When the Moon Is High

Text copyright © 2003 by Alice Schertle

Illustrations copyright © 2003 by Julia Noonan

Printed in the U.S.A. All rights reserved.

www.harperchildrens.com

Library of Congress Cataloging-in-Publication Data

Schertle, Alice.

When the moon is high / by Alice Schertle ; illustrated by Julia Noonan.

p.   cm.

Summary: A father takes his sleepless child out in the night
to see the moon and the animals.

ISBN 0-688-15143-4 — ISBN 0-688-15144-2 (lib. bdg.)

[1. Bedtime—Fiction.   2. Father and child—Fiction.   3. Moon—Fiction.

4. Animals—Fiction.   5. Stories in rhyme.]   I. Noonan, Julia, ill.   II. Title.

PZ8.3.S29717 Wh   2003   [E]—dc21   2001044632   CIP   AC

Typography by Carla Weise

1 2 3 4 5 6 7 8 9 10

First Edition

To Chad, Jody, Dave, and Ree
—A.S.

With love to my supportive father, who years
ago handed me an eight-slot plastic pencil case
in an art store in Waterbury, Connecticut, and
said, "You can fill it with any colors you like."
And with thanks to Ruth for her love and her
enthusiasm for this book.
—J.N.

Sleepy house on a sleepy hill—
all is silent, all is still.
Old Moon rises, white and round.
Not a whisper . . . not a sound. . . .

Who's that making noise? Who's calling,
tossing toys about—what's falling?

Who's that wide-awake and bawling,
"TAKE ME OUT!" when the moon is high?

Daddy's arms are warm and wide.
Someone snuggles up inside

to watch the moon wrap silver light
around the wide and wakeful night.

Who's that in a pocket peeking,
hide-and-seeking when the moon is high?

Mouse is in a pocket peeking,
hide-and-seeking when the moon is high.

Who's that on the wild wind riding,
dipping, gliding when the moon is high?

Owl is on the wild wind riding,
dipping, gliding when the moon is high.

Who's that in the bushes wrangling,
tussling, tangling when the moon is high?

Raccoon's in the bushes wrangling,
tussling, tangling when the moon is high.

Who's that snooping, getting prowly,
feeling howly when the moon is high?

Dog is snooping, getting prowly,
feeling howly when the moon is high.

Who's that like a shadow flowing,
two eyes glowing when the moon is high?

Cat is like a shadow flowing,
two eyes glowing when the moon is high.

Who's that strolling black and whitely,
tail up slightly when the moon is high?

Skunk is strolling black and whitely,
tail up slightly when the moon is high.

Who's that in the trash can munching, midnight lunching when the moon is high?

$\mathcal{P}ossum$'s in the trash can munching,
midnight lunching when the moon is high.

Shhhh!
Who's that in the darkness humming,
softly strumming when the moon is high?

Mouse out peeking,
hide-and-seeking?

Owl out riding,
dipping, gliding?

Raccoon wrangling,
tussling, tangling?

Dog out prowling,
snooping, howling?

Cat all flowing,
two eyes glowing?

Skunk out nightly,
black and whitely?

Possum munching,
midnight lunching?

Who IS humming a lullaby?

That's *Old Moon* up there softly humming,
Old Moon on the stars a-strumming
sweet dark songs. Now sleep is coming . . .

Come along!
The moon is high.